THIS BOOK BELONGS TO:

_____

LITTLE RED READING HOOD

AND THE

MISREAD WOLF

TROY WILSON

ILLUSTRATED BY **ILARIA CAMPANA**

RP | KIDS

PHILADELPHIA

To Angela Reynolds, who has forgotten more
about Little Red Riding Hood than I will ever know.

And to Shyannah, who is as smart and kind and
resourceful a niece as I could ever hope to have.

Running Press Kids
Hachette Book Group
1290 Avenue of the Americas, New York, NY 10104
www.runningpress.com/rpkids
@RP_Kids

Printed in China

First Edition: July 2019

Published by Running Press Kids, an imprint of Perseus Books,
LLC, a subsidiary of Hachette Book Group, Inc.
The Running Press Kids name and logo is a trademark of the
Hachette Book Group.

The Hachette Speakers Bureau provides a wide range of
authors for speaking events. To find out more, go to
www.hachettespeakersbureau.com or call (866) 376-6591.

The publisher is not responsible for websites (or their content)
that are not owned by the publisher.

Print book cover and interior design by Susan Van Horn.

Library of Congress Control Number: 2018948168

ISBNs: 978-0-7624-9266-4 (hardcover),
978-0-7624-9267-1 (ebook), 978-0-7624-6623-8 (ebook),
978-0-7624-6622-1 (ebook)

1010

10 9 8 7 6 5 4 3 2 1

Once there was a girl called
Little Red Reading Hood.
She loved red.
She loved reading.

And she loved the special hood
her grandma had made.

One day her grandma wasn't feeling well.

So Red made a special treat for her and set off to deliver it.

Along the way, she came across a wolf.

"Mmmm," he said, sniffing the air. "I smell my favorite smell."

Luckily, Red had read what to do if you encounter a wolf. *Maintain eye contact and slowly back away.* So she did.

The wolf kept sniffing.
And moved toward her.

Luckily, she had read what to do if a wolf moves toward you. *Stand tall, wave your arms, clap your hands, and throw rocks.* So she did.

"No, no," said the wolf, sniffing deeper and moving closer.

"I just–ouch!"

"I just want–ouch! Oh, forget it," said the wolf as he slinked away.

Red continued her journey. Along the way,
a robin asked where she was going.

Luckily, she had read what to do if a bird asks
where you're going. *Give a detailed description of your
route, while noting good spots for worms.* So she did.

Finally, Red arrived at Grandma's house.

(But the wolf had arrived first.)

Luckily, Red had read what to do if you encounter a wolf dressed as a grandparent. *Hint that you know their secret by pointing out their big features.* So she did.

"What a big nose you have," she said.

"All the better to smell my favorite smell—er, I mean smell every smell," replied the wolf.

He resisted the urge to sniff.

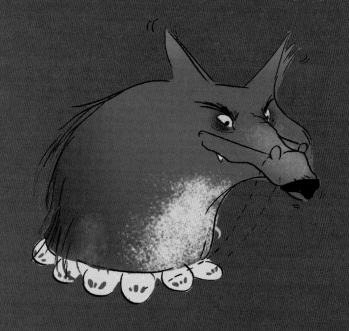

"What big ears you have," she said.
"All the better to hear every
word." He really wanted to sniff.

"What big eyes you have."
"All the better to see every picture."
He really, really wanted to sniff.

"What big teeth you have."
"All the better—" He sniffed. "All the
better to—" He sniff-sniff-sniffed.

"Oh, forget it!" said
the wolf as he pounced.

Luckily, Red had read what to do if a wolf dressed as a grandparent pounces. *Shout and swing an axe.* Unluckily, she didn't have an axe. And her shouting sounded more like screaming.

Red ran for the kitchen.
The wolf didn't waste a second.

His big jaws
yanked the treat
out of the basket.

"Will you read this to me?"
"Where's Grandma?!"
demanded Red.
"But I *am* Grandma."

"WHERE'S GRANDMA?!!!!"

"But . . . but . . . no one ever reads to me," said the wolf. "Will you read to me? Please?"

She had never read what to do if a wolf sniffs the book you made for Grandma, asks you to read it, and doesn't once try to eat you.

But Red did know that you can't judge a book by its cover.

"Okay," she said. "If you bring me Grandma, I will read to both of you."

So he did.

And luckily . . .

. . . they *all* loved books.